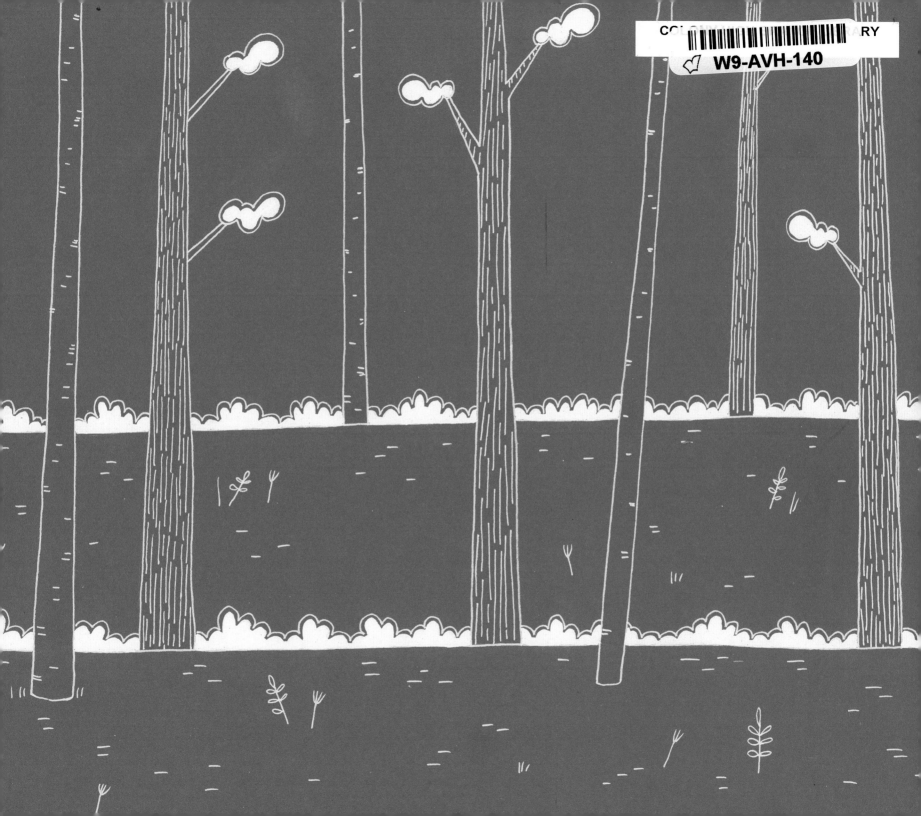

A HORSE NAMED Steve

FOR *Ella, Katie* AND *Greta.*

AND IN MEMORY OF *Ellis* ... THANKS FOR THE INSPIRATION.

Kids Can Press gratefully acknowledges the financial support of the Government of Ontario, through the Ontario Media Development Corporation; the Ontario Arts Council; the Canada Council for the Arts; and the Government of Canada, through the CBF, for our publishing activity.

Published in Canada and the U.S. by Kids Can Press Ltd.
25 Dockside Drive, Toronto, ON M5A 0B5

www.kidscanpress.com

Kids Can Press is a Corus Entertainment Inc. company

The artwork in this book was rendered in ink and watercolor, and finished in Photoshop.
The text is set in Lemon Yellow Sun and Mulberry Script Pro.

Edited by Yasemin Uçar
Designed by Karen Powers

Printed and bound in Shenzhen, China, in 10/2016 by C&C Offset.

CM 17 0 9 8 7 6 5 4 3 2 1

LIBRARY AND ARCHIVES CANADA CATALOGUING IN PUBLICATION

Collier, Kelly (Kelly M.), author, illustrator
A horse named Steve / written and illustrated by Kelly Collier.

ISBN 978-1-77138-736-1 (hardback)

I. Title.

PS8605.O458H67 2017   jC813'.6   C2016-902600-0

A HORSE NAMED Steve

WRITTEN AND ILLUSTRATED BY **KELLY COLLIER**

KIDS CAN PRESS

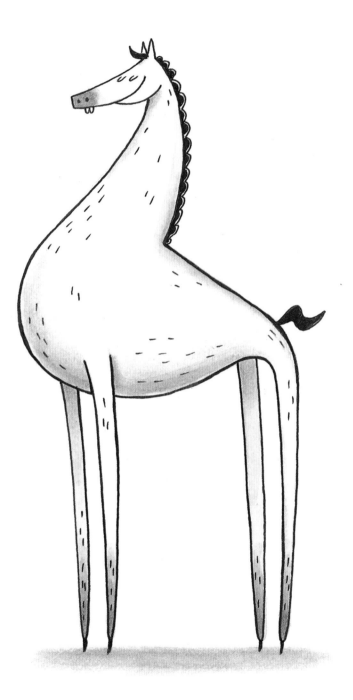

THIS IS *Steve*.

Steve IS A FINE HORSE.
BUT HE THINKS
HE COULD BE FINER.

HE WANTS TO BE
EXCEPTIONAL.

THAT MEANS SPECIAL.

Steve HAS HEARD THAT SOME HORSES GET TO WEAR RIBBONS!

SIGH

WOOT
WOOT

AND THEN *Steve* KNOWS
THIS HORN WILL MAKE HIM
EXCEPTIONAL.

CLAP
CLAP
CLAP

Steve STRAPS THE HORN TO HIS HEAD ...

HMMMMMM ...

TOO BAD STEVE'S
HORN DIDN'T COME
WITH VELCRO.

OVER, UNDER, AROUND
AND THROUGH.

... AND GALLOPS OFF TO SHOW HIS FRIENDS.

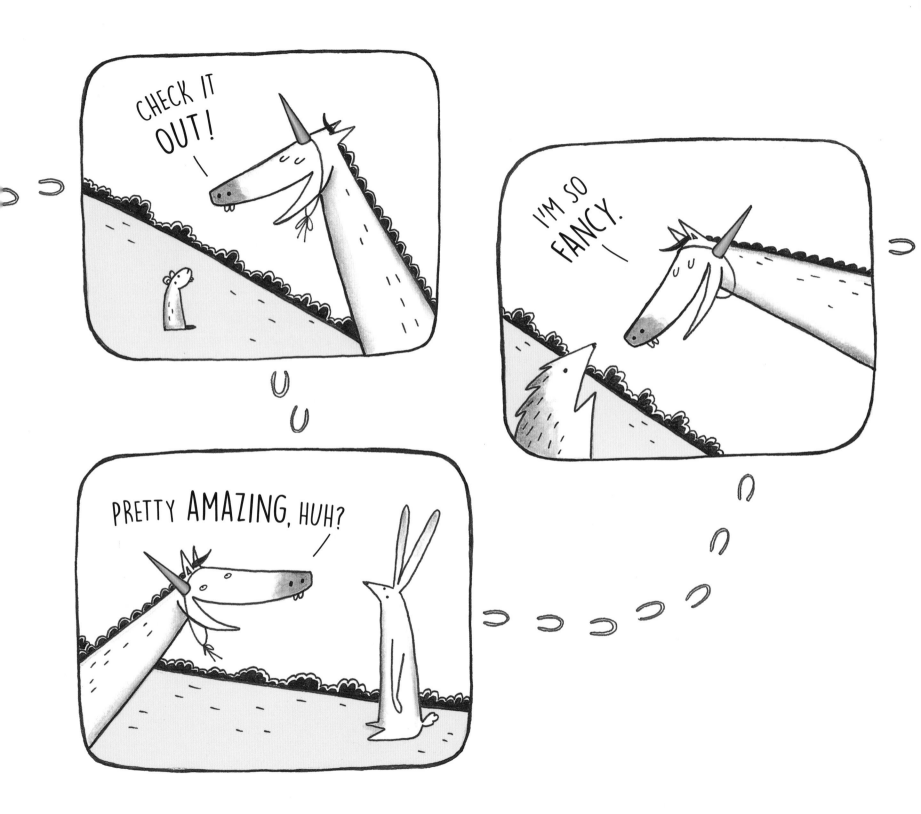

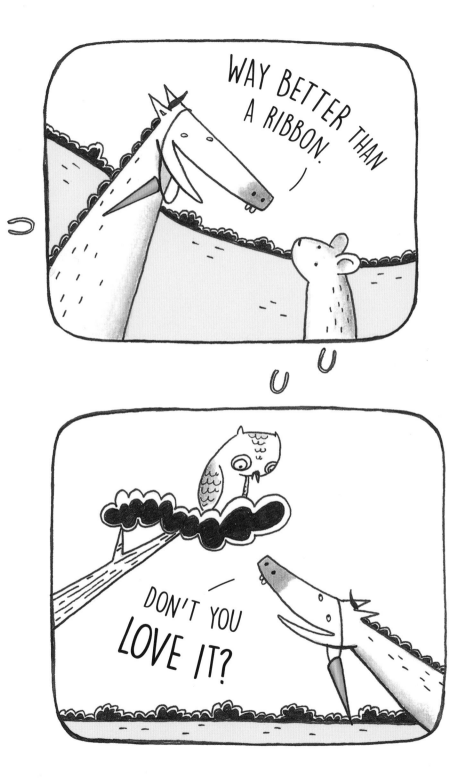

"... SO I JUST SAW IT AND THOUGHT, Steve, YOU COULD REALLY DO SOMETHING WITH THIS. AND I'M SO GLAD I DID, BECAUSE I'M AN EXCEPTIONAL HORSE NOW. BOB, YOU SHOULD REALLY FIND A HORN, TOO, BECAUSE YOU'RE LOOKING KIND OF ORDINARY ..."

"BUT STEVE," SAYS BOB, "I DON'T SEE A BEAUTIFUL GOLD HORN ON YOUR HEAD. YOU ARE NOT EXCEPTIONAL!"

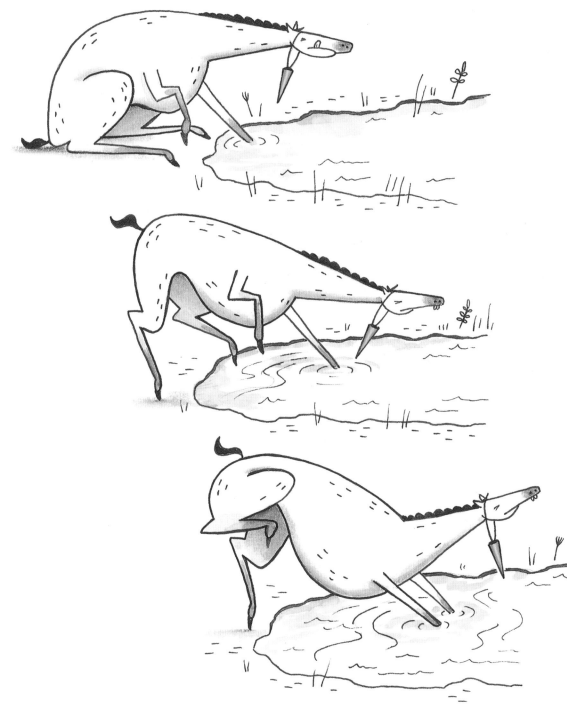

Steve REACHES FOR HIS HORN, BUT HE CAN'T QUITE GRASP IT.

SO HE REACHES FARTHER ...

AND THEN A WEE BIT FARTHER ...

AND NOW HIS FRIENDS HAVE **SPECIAL THINGS** STRAPPED TO THEIR HEADS AND HE DOESN'T!

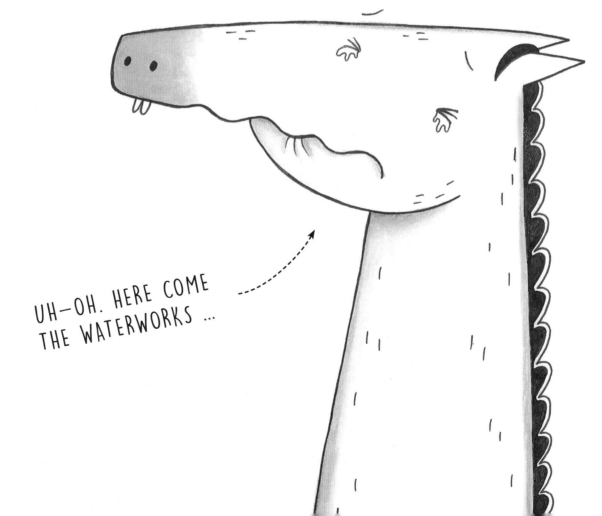

UH—OH. HERE COME THE WATERWORKS ...

Steve

HE IS SUCH A
TRENDSETTER, THIS GUY.

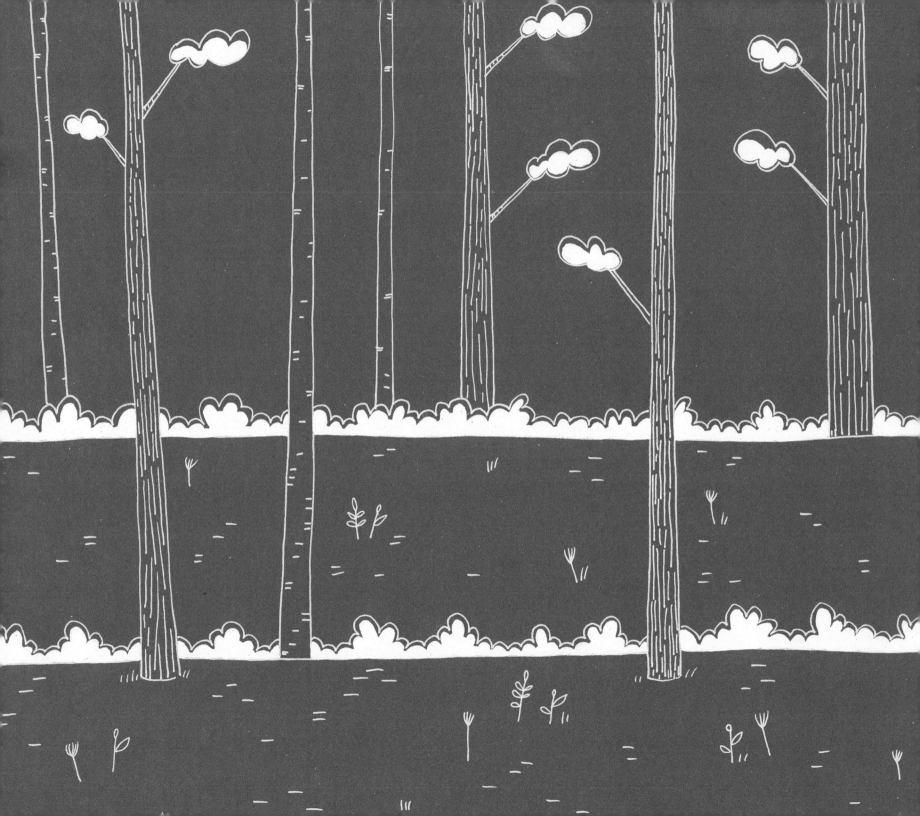